CHILD

OF A

STOLEN LAND

PAUL BURROUGHS

DEDICATION

All powerful praise to the Most High and all the Heavens for preciously
protecting me during my most testing troubling terrible times.

CHAPTER 1

Gossiping trees whispered in the dead of the night as a colony of thirsty vampire bats raided the warm night. A black panther prince blended in the dark while mirroring his father from afar. Their radiating eyes came to life in the dark, like golden fiery orbs that could be seen from afar. Crystal clear pods of night dew splashed down on the rich ground as the stealthy black king crept with no sound. An unmindful herd of elegant red deer burned in the humid night, while grazing in plain sight. A wave of murderous thoughts flooded the elusive feline's mind as he gracefully prowled through frozen time. The treacherous grass cushioned the deadly hunter's gentle paw every time in desperate hope of his enemies' timely demise. Sangre trickled down the ebony doe's succulent thigh as tiny vampires attempted to drain her dry. A blind full moon watched from the clear night sky, for thousands of stars served as his eyes. The gluttonous female deer grazed away at the tempting lush grass, still unaware of the bat winged demons attached.

"I desire to be strong like no other, since my only role model is my father," the crouching cub whispered while learning a valuable lesson in the wild night.

Startled sleeping baboons screamed out abruptly within the sinful night as a herd of passion red deer flickered out of sight. A homeless soul wandered aimlessly into the humid night before being uplifted atop the starry-eyed sky. The gentle doe-eyed spirit galloped up a sacred staircase as it followed the light to the Great Beyond. Blood dripped from the tongue of a remorseful killer, for many don't realize death is no thriller.

"Pardis! Come here, my only son, so you may understand the burden of the burning sun. Death creeps in the night, since silent killers prefer to move out of sight. The mighty sun's job is never done, as the battle of good versus evil rages on. Its purifying beams of light thaw the freezing soul, detoxing the land of a murderous night cold. Do not believe others, for they hath not been told of the secrets that you'll behold. We only kill for a meal, since peace watches from atop the great hill. The never-ending web of life is a precious deal, which is why we honor those whom we've killed. The sun scorns the creatures of the night, who sends us seeking the shelter of the masking night. Mutilated bodies and half-eaten corpses litter this dark land until the mourning sun burn their empty bodies to scattering ash. The doe who lies here lifeless lived a life that was priceless. We as the guardians of this divine land thrive off the flesh of an innocent demand. Value no life over another, not even your own, my beloved black prince. Feast upon her flesh in sadness, for now she exists no more in this realm. Honor the death of every creature, as no life should ever outshine another. Do you comprehend these wise words, my dear Pardis?" the black king voiced to his precious son, who glowed under the night sun.

"I overstand your sane words, Father, for my desire is to become great like you. My ears will listen, as my body shall move to only the path which you approve. I'm nothing more than a shapeless stone, who awaits to be sculpted by the hands of your own. You as my father must mold me into an image greater than your own, as you're the black king and I'm the shadow prince who must one day claim the lonely throne. Now I feast in the mighty name of my all-powerful father. Who stands over my supreme father? I shall answer thee myself, for no creation can defeat my almighty father. Let us feast in sorrow, Father, as our hearts beat to the vibrations of the overseeing full moon," the wide-eyed golden orb midnight cub voiced with great pride as he began to feast at his father's humble side.

"Do not consume her flesh, for I must teach you a brief lesson. Who created me, Pardis?" the sitting wise panther growled while looking over at his confused son.

"What have I done, dear Father?" the cub asked calmly.

"Who created me my beloved son?" the black king said sternly while staring up at the night burning sun.

"We are all created equal in the eyes of the Most High, who promise our souls shall never die. Why do you ask? You taught me those words before I could even see in this beautiful world," Pardis purred to his listening father.

"Listen to me, young prince, as I know new souls can be quite dense. Your purpose is to serve Him, as you've embodied the divine image of the Great One. A child of a God but not by me. For there is only one Creator but many imitators who claim to be divine dictators. Do not worship thy parents, for we are all equal within the gates of everlasting peace. The walls of my heart protect every part of your fragile soul, but my job merely is to show you the road. I'm your father on earth but a guardian blood brother in the realm of angels. Give thanks to the Great One, who watches over this world night and day. Never praise a creature, who shall die someday. Only give praise to thee that hath giveth breath to your body every day of your life, for He is the one that has guided and protected you in this unforgiving world. I'm your teacher, who teaches from the heart. I'm your winged guardian, who protects you from the start. You shall learn much from me, son, but even after death, my job will not be done. For my spirit may guide and protect you for eternal life, may we grow old together and witness many births, my son. A father will never leave their children to struggle in this dehumanized mess of a world. Do you understand, my beloved son?" the black king voiced deeply before closing the eyes of an innocent victim cast to the calming belly of the self-eating serpent.

"I overstand your wise words, my honorable father, so forgive me as a son who'll work harder. The Great One knows my pure heart desires only to please my ancestors, who've watched over me from the start. I do not even feel worthy to even speak to the Most High, which is why with Him I did not start. If you decide to wonder why, Father, then this is the answer on my part. Just to let you know that your treasured shadow prince means no offense, for my heart has yearned to be close to Him since my eyes first blinked," Pardis said sincerely to his attentive father.

"Pardis, listen to me, my only son, for I fear death is on the run in the distance. You must learn faster than the quickest of lightning, for death comes in the night with no sightings. Your ears must grab my words faster than the rat cursed race can run. For I sense their foul presence in the near future to come, so now is no time to be dumb, my son. The Most High deserves all of your praise, for your ancestors serve the divine creator. Without Him, we cease to exist, along with every other creation whom He has created. The ancestors are very much appreciated because they serve as our guides and guardians in this life. We are only visitors, who must protect the Creator's divine creations. Your purpose is to serve the Most High, even if it means that you must die. Never live a lie, as you're meant to die for the future of your people. Walk the path He places you on, for that is the one your destiny lies on. Once my time comes, then I shall walk by your side unseen. For I'm your deathless guardian, who shall guide and shield you in the Great Beyond. But fear not, for if my death comes before you're old, then just know that I'll be there by your side. Your pure heart will be tainted with hatred, but a foreign being shall purify the poisoned waters. Keep your eyes open for this special individual, for her eyes will resemble the North Star shining in the night blue sky. For she is a diamond forged by a gentle fire, which makes her shine differently among her cold people. Protect this beautiful soul, as she will be the key to your salvation. Do you understand my wise words, Pardis?" the black king said before being alerted by heavy galloping feet.

"I overstand your wise words, my beloved father. Is everything okay? For it seems as if you've been alarmed by something utmost alarming. Forgive my curious nature, Father, but my inner concern is worried about you. Father?" the anxious Negro cub remarked with utmost concern.

"Death is about to make its grand entrance, for I've been summoned as a valued chess piece on the board of eternal life. You must remain strong, for the storm has arrived in the shadow of the calm night. Listen to your heart and allow the guardian spirits to lead your wandering soul to a hidden divine paradise. Do you understand, my only son?" the black king replied as a towering red deer trotted over the two golden-eyed shadow cats.

"I overstand your wise words, Father, for destruction has polluted our pure land. The air travels with a familiar scent, which mirrors that of innocent blood. I sense a great storm looming over our heads, as death values nothing of having dear friends. Now my mouth will shut while I listen to kings converse in the restless night," Pardis said to his powerful father, who stood facing the oncoming mighty antlered herd leader.

A flaming stag towered over the strong shadow king whose eyes flickered with an undying flame. The stars whispered of a great treachery, which has burned through the sacred valleys of the land. Messengers of the night howled to the spirits, who lay their heads on the dark side of the moon. Hyenas laughed at the viper for trading his legs for poison, for now the serpent could no longer walk the earth. A chorus of calming crickets calmed the startled wind, as rain fell from the restless sky. Smoke rose in the distance, for a fire burned with resistance. The trees began to uproot from the rich ground without even a mere sound. For trouble has fallen from the dark side of the great rock, which once burned like the mind of a man who cannot talk. A sea of invasive black rats flooded the empty forest floor before being pushed back into shadows by the black king's mighty roar. Their beady eyes burned with hatred as they scurried toward the destructive flames. Blood poured from the bodies of the guiltless, while bone-chilling cries of screaming rape victims traumatized the bloody night. Plummeting burning rocks fell from the sleeping heavens, which carried a cursed race of beings who awakened a dormant plague of rats. Fear trembled the mighty red stag's voice as he spoke to the worried black panther.

"Do not fear me, brother deer, for I only kill your sick, injured, or old. My spirit has guided this sick soul to the healing hands of the Creator so someday she can return free of disease and pain," the black king said with compassion.

"I fear you not, my black king, for you are a powerful leader who protects this sacred land. My kind are honored to nourish the bodies of the shifters of the night, for they keep peace between the humans and the untamed wildlife. We have coexisted in this realm since the beginning of time. But now a great evil has fallen down upon us, which will destroy the indigenous of this world. We must fight these destructive invaders, for the storm has arrived in the sweltering night. The spirit of my herd burns with retaliation as they wait in the uprooted footprints of the traveling trees. We wait on the call of your command, my black king, as we are prepared to fight for the peace of this land," the monstrous stag grunted while gesturing toward the Negro panther.

"The rat has no honor, for in desperate times, it shall turn on its kin. A reborn snake sheds its old skin after digesting the body of the deceitful rodent. I am a loyal servant of the Creator, otherwise the known shepherd of this exotic pasture. So I must give my life in return for the safety of my meek people. Take my son with you to the paradise hidden beneath the skin of the earth after calling your people to safety at once. The meek creatures of that forgotten land shall embrace your arrival with love and immediate care. Command your army of prideful bucks to return with the warm bodies of the stranded and weary-hearted. Do you understand my wise words, beloved brother deer?" the shadow cat growled.

"I overstand your wise words, my black king. Return my royal crowned warriors, for we must rescue the guiltless and flee to the paradise beneath the skin of the earth," the burning hart grunted lowly while telepathically communicating with his listening herd at the tap of his feet.

"Please forgive me, Pardis, for I shall return in spirit. You will never be alone, for we are immortal, my son. Fear not, for the angels watch over while you stumble in this mine-infested land. Death shall not come prematurely to you nor to those who reside in your heart, my beloved son. You must retreat now, so then your strength may grow with time and much-needed love. Only you can command the storm to end after leading the meek to a hidden sanctuary, my dear son. My love is eternal, just like my warrior spirit," the royal shadow cat voiced deeply before bounding off into the raging fire-lit night.

Burning stars fell from ocean as a blanket of darkness covered Mother Earth's nighttime ceiling.

The stampede of fiery-hearted bucks quaked the night before the accursed creatures arose from their flaming rocks. A nighthawk soared high above the plagued land while clutching a precious stone in its fearsome talons. Rescued animals screamed in horror as they rode atop the dashing bucks. Rat-tailed humanoids exited their cooled rock capsules before revealing their gray-scaled skin. Their burning red eyes viewed the land with hatred as they thrashed the ferocious panther with flaming whips. Falling stars riddled the soft earth as hundreds of foreign invaders attacked the deadly attacking black king. The shape-shifting king shifted into a powerful black dragon, who devoured his enemies in unimaginable numbers. Burning whips did little damage to the tough feather-scaled cockatrice, who battled fiercely for the timely retreat of his people. The tall grey-scaled invaders' empty faces slowly began to sprout the face of lost creatures. Their long elongated arms bore claws like that of a grizzly as they wore the face of beautiful men and women. Sharp teeth ripped into the hot flesh of the fire-breathing cockatrice as alien monsters ripped off the dragon's protective armor. The death-screaming dragon called the help of Death as it scorched the land with a screeching torch of flames.

"I will always honor you, Father, for I've learned many lessons in your presence. You have showed me the way of a warrior, which means I must die in service of the Creator's people as well," the teary-eyed shadow prince said softly while being carried away into the swallowing darkness by a guardian eagle owl.

CHAPTER 2

A furious fire forged the forsaken landscape until the land was naked like a fresh sword. Flaming rocks continued to plummet down from the smothered sky as smoke concealed the foreign beings who walked in disguise. Enslaved villagers' pained eyes filled with raw fear as they witnessed their loved ones slain like innocent deer. Devilish screams muffled the sorrowful cries of grieving orphans, who snuggled next to slaughtered corpses. The humanoid invaders resembled mere mortals as they attempted to acclimate themselves to this new planet. Their features became that of a person, all except for a few distinct differences.

"All of our skin remains grey as the tail chooses to stay. Being human is such a waste, anyway, but luckily my emotions have stayed away. Most mortals lack being human almost every day every time the sun turns its attention away. How long must we stay on this peaceful planet, anyway, my fellow Aduboola? For we've conquered many realms and far worlds, but I see not our actions as good deeds. As I view them to be our very own demise, for this foreign sensation speaks to me. And it warns of a lone survivor, who shall put an end to our wrongdoings. That beast could have destroyed the entire colony if we would've refused to inject our much-needed serum. For we have not the ability to tolerate the sun of any planet, nor the heat can none of us even withstand. But our technology is advanced, and we defy Death itself, as we drain the life force from every planet and enslave the race who depends on it.

"The mountain built on the backs of slaves shall fall once one stands up, and then others will follow. Self-proclaimed kings will fall, and the savages we've enslaved shall tear us limb from limb. I find this feeling to be justified, for I'm not proud of my existence. A mountain will always crumble from the bottom once the awakened land stomach starts to rumble. We were blessed with technology but cursed just like humanity. Why must we continue this legacy of utmost insanity? Do we not live in a reality of that we must die? Despite our extended years, which is only due to our forbidden technology, we pride ourselves as being of the Aduboola, but none of us know where we go after we've exhausted our unique bodies. We huddle children into cramped cages, like animals to the slaughter.

Their surviving parents shall be enslaved. Meanwhile, these sweet children will become mindless servants to our race. How would we like our offspring being abused and tortured in the most inhumane way until their mind leaves the body? The seed we plant on this planet shall not be a harvest we desire to reap. Answer me, my fellow Aduboola, for I demand you as a soldier who serves beneath me!" the senior Aduboola said passionately to his younger subordinate while rustling up *chiquito* brown and Negro children from atop the backs of invisible beast.

Burning whips crackled in the suffocating air as Aduboola gathered their prized cattle into electrifying cages. Their eyes were white, for not even rage showed inside, such foul creatures driven by a foolish pride. For their curse is why they ran, for the sun they cannot withstand. As their serum is not made by man but processed by foreigners, who harvest life-bearing lands.

Their long-limbed bodies straddled the invisible monsters, which shimmered in the fiery night. Flames glimmered under the burning sky as star angels revealed the creatures' identity to the untrained eye. Feathered reptiles who wore armored scales underneath wreaked havoc as they bled the night with murderous sight. Stars continued to fall in the distance as unseen beast hunted and devoured escaping villagers. Fire burned in their eyes as dreams burned in the background. Nightmares come to life on a page, which how faux history is taught to this naive age. For many of us have lived many lives before this illusion of time. Focus on words but ride to the rhyme. Question everything, for the answer lies within inside you, as no stone shall be left unturned once the Creator returns after devastation. The creatures resemble a bizarre creation as it walked with an ancient sensation. Harpy eagle talons equipped the invisible beast feet while running swiftly and silently after sure-footed human prey. A series of high-pitched clicks relayed complex messages back and forth as the lizard-faced wolves worked together to silence screaming prey. Giant flaming rocks cooled on the petrified ground as fear blew a cold wind across the fearful land. Aduboola soldiers cracked open their frozen rocks with large hands before exiting the spacecraft and quickly taking a deceiving form. Their rat tails held high as they watched the chaos through windows of an empty soul. Fallen rock turned into forbidden structures, which hid in lectures for the fool's pleasure. A vast town sprouted into its early form as poison hardened the pure ground. Roads were paved as stubborn trees slowly withered away. The ghost monsters carried cages of children and other prisoners, who dangled from their short powerful arms. A sorrowful moon could cry no more, as the sky ran out of tears.

Settling rain had no effect on the manipulated native fire spirit until his power became a mere annoyance. Fire-suppressing chemicals attacked the confused fiery spirit, who wandered aimlessly about the burn-proof town. The flaming wild spirit burned with rage until being calmed by the gentle wind spirit, who knew retreat was best. Night and Day children were forced into rat-infested prison as adults were stripped naked and chained in center of town. Before they tested on rats, the experiment was us.

"Mother! Why do they hurt us? Is it because peace sets on the mountains and calmness spews from the youthful fountains? Mother! Why do they take away our parents but raise their own in safety of a bleached world? Mother! Please help me, for Father lies dead on the floor before my feet! I tell this alien devil, but no sense enters his brain. This mask-wearing demon beats me until I see bloody bone! I was born a free soul, and unchained we all shall go! Forgive me, Mother, for I must attempt to free us both and get all back home!" a young native earth colored voiced with an endless flow of moving tears, which shook the dying father from the grasp of Death.

Evil black hat rats gathered within the prison walls as they plotted their villainous plan for mass consumption. Both fellow soldiers continued to converse despite the fighting young girl, who ignored her loving mother's desperate cries of reason. Anger boiled beneath the skin of the lower-ranking soldier once the conversation was abruptly ended by his frustrated superior.

"Mother! I fight to be free from these foreign oppressors, for I'm a bird of no cage! May my dream come true one day, as I wish my people can live in peace once again. We shall be together once more my warmhearted mother!" the ebony-skinned girl said in a fight for freedom as she struggled to climb over the alien human imposters.

"Get off of me, you filthy slave, who has not washed your skin! Die on the pavement like a bleeding animal, who has no purpose in the universe. Why does she wear such black and grotesque skin?" the lower-ranking soldier said aloud irritably after slamming the flailing night girl onto sangre-stained prison pavement.

"Why would you do such a thing, Sax!" the superior Aduboola responded angrily.

"Get over it because it sounds like you're falling for these filthy savages. Have you forgotten the reason we've came to this resourceful planet?" Sax asked in a disrespectful tone to his superior before being stabbed in the back by a resurrected black father, who had witnessed the senseless death of his precious daughter.

A web of bloody rivers flooded the stone floor as life gushed from the innocent child's cracked head. Blood rushed from her head like a freed yolk from a cracked egg. The indigo blue night sky faded within a once lively young girl, who had spent her day plucking flowers from the lush meadow. Her indigo eyes went white before her body melted to ash. A calming wind mourned the physical loss as she guided the lost spirit across her past life. Top hat black rats harvested the girl's organs as her father repeatedly stabbed her murderer in his back.

"Tomu! Watch out, my love, for the creature clings to the edge of life! Turn around, my brave husband, as the tail prepares for attack! Tomu, hear me now!" the distressed ebony wife screamed out to her in shock husband before watching him being pierced through the heart by the monster's piercing tail.

"You have no honor, Sax, for he returned in order to save his baby girl. Your death was guaranteed due to the severity of inflicted wounds, and you continued to take this man's life. Why?" the superior Aduboola voiced with pain while watching his comrade collapse to the ground and releasing a lodged weaponized tail.

"Lox, you've been living a dream ever since that damned daughter of yours was born. I've watched my leader become soft and committing thoughts of treason against his own people. My death has honor, for I die by the code of a true Aduboola. Your daughter is a curse to this colony, but I must go now, as I would scream for assistance, since you pose a threat to our mission. But I prefer you to struggle raising that worthless daughter, who will never be accepted by others like me. My last words shall haunt you for eternity because a death by the colony is far more deserving, Sergeant Lox. You care more for the slaves we harvest than your own kind. Are you even an Aduboola? For we live for ourselves and only care for each other. As we are greedy and can become drunk with power. We are a conquering race, who have conquered nothing but silly stories of a supreme Creator, who created all creations. They are primitive and must be put to great use before dying their simple senseless lives. I laugh at Death, for I am my own creator," Sax relayed harshly before coughing up all of his alien organs atop the blood-covered prison floor.

"Why do you bleed red, Sax? Their beliefs could be the answer to breaking our curse because have become delusional monsters who destroy peace in the land. You killed a father and daughter and leave that poor crying Negra to die in even more sorrow of knowing her family is dead. But I don't know because death sounds better than being experimented on and enslaved.

"We harvest their spirits to strengthen our weak souls as the curse drains our skin of our natural color and feeds on our existence. Peace once ruled the Darkest Valley of the Moon, which is our native homeland. Until famine and disease struck our land, causing the planet to have undesirable living conditions. Our moon mirrored the earth and was once called the Mirroring Twin Planets. Both planets thrived with the blessing of life until we began worshipping ourselves and abusing resources of a peaceful world. We once worshipped a supreme God, very much similar to every indigenous we've encountered. We called Him the Great One of the universe, but that changed once our corrupt leaders reshaped His image to mirror their mental portrayal. The Aduboola were once like these people until our leaders accepted forbidden devices from an unspoken dark force, forever cursing our mere existence, for we are nothing but slaves tricked into slavery by false promises of greed and power. Our puppet masters laugh as we do their bidding and take the blame for such hideous crimes.

"You are a fool in disguise who fights for nothing but the bullshit which he is fed to us. Rat DNA was spliced into our own, so we must survive and hopefully adapt like the sneaky rodents. But instead our lifespan was shortened, similar to those flea-carrying vermin. We have been rocked to sleep and now refuse to wake up for the potion is what we take in. We must infest these beautiful worlds because peace and emotion have been bred out of our genetic makeup. Nothing but mere puppets, who sit on standby for a hidden force unseen to simple beings. We are plagued rats of a foreign land, who cannot coexist with no creation. As we the Aduboola have lost our way, I fear we'll all reap a catastrophic harvest one day. I'm done speaking to you, heathen, for my family will not abide by these laws. For one day we shall assist in the fall of the Aduboola, who believe no Higher Power exist except themselves. That widowed night woman shall find shelter and love under my roof until the Great One of the universe gives me a sign to act on my heart furthermore. So before you explode with rage and reveal my intentions, understand that I must take your head, heathen," Lox voiced calmly right before smashing the fellow soldier's grey shaved morphed human head with a single deadly stomp into the quaking prison floor.

A violent gang of invisible beast pursued a patriotic herd of fleeing deer, who flickered across the ashen landscape. The retreating warriors pushed their limits as they raced toward the remaining stretch of enchanted forest. Cold-blooded predators hawked down their unwary prey until distance could no longer keep their snapping jaws at bay. Harsh cries echoed in the black of night as Mother Earth's children scrambled to escape a frenzy of unseen prehistoric killers. Frightened forest critters vanished into the ancient forest. Meanwhile, a staggering stag tossed a screaming shadow cub. Maternal tree branches caught the falling feline before reaching out to save the injured mature buck.

"Get him to safety, for I choose to die on the battlefield with my fellow brothers. A barrier must be set in place before these murderous beings destroy our magical home! Pardis, you shall bring down these monsters as you grow to be more powerful than your great father! To die fighting is an honor, for my spirit will run this land forever!" the bloody stag grunted aloud before being torn apart by vicious invisible beast who could not breach the enchanted barrier.

CHAPTER 3

La familia of roaming elephants woke the earth as they fed alongside the enchanted barrier. Rat-tailed imposters went about their busy lives while using the land's resources at an alarming rate. Various scientists studied the indigo barrier. Meanwhile, a team of special operations made many failed attempts to infiltrate the other side. The white-eyed, pale-skinned monster's eyes gleamed red as the sun scorned their way of life. Aduboolas came to Earth prepared for the eye in the burning sky as science has given them a false upper hand to survive.

Wild dholes patrolled in large packs atop the grass-covered ground while searching the enclosed forest for potential prey. A lone black wolf paced frantically back and forth as he waited for the great stone door to open. Elephants sensed the vibrations underground as a forgotten prince emerged from the shadows. Weeping tree roots nourished the shape-shifting orphan until he reached the age of abandoned angel children. Eleven years living underground caused the anxious Negro wolf to impatiently squeeze between the sliding rock. Bright light blinded the boisterous shadow wolf, who wiped his golden eyes with monstrous paws.

A maternal tree gave a helping hand as she cried tears of joy and wiped away the whining wolf child's painful blindness. The Negro lobo was raised in the darkness, so walking in the light was the hardest. A boy raised by a loving tree spirit, who watched over the abandoned star child. She was respected by all creatures of the world, except by the current plague of destructive Aduboola. These unpeaceful beings worked day and night nonstop as they performed countless attempts to break the barrier around the clock.

"You must walk in the footsteps of your father, for now the shadow fades as the light of a king shines down upon you." An old tree spirit rustled in the calming wind as she watched her beloved son view the beauty of the natural world once again.

"The North Star guides me to my destination, for my people await their emancipation. For I must leave the barrier in my human form once a blanket of darkness covers the sleeping sun. But as of now, I shall patrol the shadows of my protected land until sacred night stars crown this body as a black king. Do not fear, Mother

Tree, for this is how the ancestors decided it to be. So rest easy, my beloved mother, as my life will be long for. I'm immortal since wholeheartedly I believe so, which means I shall never cease to be alive nor those who reside within my heart will never die. A full moon sits high as an owl soars by in the stab wound sky. For is the universe nothing but a mere child only seeking to pry with only curious eyes, who poke holes in the sky with a dulled blade knife. For I am life, as my eyes see the vision of the Most High. Question not I but ask thyself for who sits high and bless thee with wealth. Do not say him, be cursed you say thyself, for I tell your ignorant minds myself. For thou all living lives in wealth themselves, as this life is your chance to save themselves. Those blessed with wealth of this world, who were most given by the Most High shall die a life of misery a thousand times. A land built on the backs of the enslaved washes away in blood once life washes its hands of wicked man. My love grows with you, Mother Tree, which is why I must bring salvation to our stolen land," the young wolf voiced passionately to his earthly mother before bounding off deeper into an ancient forest.

"You possess the eyes of the Creator, who created the universe and all the creations contained within. The blessing of the stars touched you at birth, which means you've been chosen by the Most High. May my watchful spirit watch over you as the ancestors guide and protect your forsaken soul. Pardis, you've trained underground for eleven years ever since you turned eight, and your father was slain by those despicable colonizers. Change will come, so be patient, my children," Mother Tree said softly before sensing a great disturbance amid the waking forest community.

Waking skies blessed the jungle with life as the sun fully opened its bright burning eyes. Red-furred savages squabbled over breakfast as tazzy black devils squalled in the bloody background. An armed pack of angry dholes attacked the tazzy maniacs, who cried over being bullied off the freshly departed baby elephant carcass. A feeding frenzy of razor-sharp teeth butchered several tazzy devils as they attempted to feed on the dead ivory prince. Exotic parrots gossiped from within the trees as hummingbirds whispered to pollinating bees. Blood stained the wings of tiger-striped monarchs, who rested atop scarlet red camellias. Elder trees watched in sadness as madness raided the minds of once innocent minds. The praying trees swayed in a circle as they encircled both fighting sides. A family of quail scurried to the side as a dark wolf raced out of the shaded forest and into the sunburned clearing.

"Stop the madness, fellow brothers, for this is not our ways, my brethren. We are this world's warriors, who must not lose our way. Be grateful for the sacrifice of this baby elephant, as now you and your families' stomach will be filled. Do not disrespect the dead, especially those who nourished your body. For sickness may fall down upon those who consume the flesh of the tortured and neglected, as karma sees fit to insult those that betrayed her. Join me as we feast in sorrow but give thanks to the Most High for a life we've borrowed. Come now, my brothers, as we share this nourishing meal," the Negro wolf voiced passionately before lowering his large head to bite a chunk out of the death-given meal.

"Death feeds the creatures of this planet by taking a soul and giving it to another who takes life for granted. Green grass could live a long life as the wild hair of Mother Earth, but grazing deer and plant-eating kin prefer to consume her living hair, only so they can live to die in despair. I show no mercy because no mercy was shown to me. Our families were killed by those damned colonizers, and now insanity drives my actions. Starvation sets in the eyes of the sun, as our natural prey is far too low to hunt or already gone. We lived in harmony for years, but their forbidden technology is causing us to turn on each other. Who might you be, anyway, to tell us how to live, stranger? For your scent is unfamiliar, so I hope that you belong here, brother. Because we've all eaten our cub brothers once food became scarce and parents turned selfish. I've never had a black wolf before, especially since they first disappeared eleven years ago. You should run shadow wolf because a mad hunger rages within me!" the dholes' crazed chief exclaimed madly before leading the pack on an organized rampage aimed toward a lone black wolf.

"Who are you to question I?" the wolf asked the chief sternly.

"I am the pack leader my wolf brother and also top dog around these parts nowadays!" the chief yelled before viciously lunging at his shadowy target.

"Only a fool believes he owns the land, as a wise man knows life is fragile and sits in our hands," The wolf growled before shifting into a swift black mamba and delivering a deadly flow of neurotoxin venom inside the raging chief's airlifted body.

"That is no wolf, so don't be fooled!" growled a red savage, who took charge of the pack after watching life vacate the chief's body.

"What are you doing, Kane? My life continues to hold on in this world, so I'm still in charge of this pack. Step down now, Kane! This treachery is not like you, for we are blood brothers. I do not wish to hurt thee, Kane, so please step down," the chief growled as the sun gave him strength to witness his brother's gut-wrenching betrayal.

"You wish not to hurt thyself, for poison courses through the veins of a dying dog. I crown myself king while watching my brother die. So pass on now, peasant, for we shall consume you and this creature of unknown origin. Just lie down and die, like the groveling mutt you were cursed to be, my dear Bane," Kane snarled to his staggering brother, who collapsed right before a heartless sibling.

"Allow me to help you, brother, for I love thee like no other. As I really hate to see you suffer and listen to my hungry stomach make these empty complaints to a frozen heart. My spirit burns now with hate, as now I choose to take thy life for self's sake!" Kane snarled to his teary-eyed brother.

"I truly love you, Kane, for my heart could never do harm unto another brother," Bane voiced sincerely before being silenced like a screaming lamb in the wolf's den.

Blood trickled down Kane's muzzle as he ripped out his brother's throat and fellow pack members consumed the corpse's raw entrails. A blind black coyote cried to a blinding sun because this gifted heaven is no more a place of peace. Not even among the animals, for the foul ways of man have even tainted their pure souls. The trees whispered death throughout a grieving forest as a crying wind whined a whistling tune. Clouds fled their deep blue pastures as cannibalistic canines cried bloody murder to the clear skies. A slithering serpent went unnoticed as he silently injected all of the starving savages with a deadly sickness. Their blood pressure skyrocketed as red tears soaked their burning red fur. The fire within them grew faint as light dimmed in their eyes. A dark-scaled mamba stood above its enemies' poisoned bodies before morphing into a black butterfly and fluttering off on a trail of sorrow.

CHAPTER 4

Black devils danced in the deep shadows as dark bodies hung deeply from rooted gallows. Soaring vultures casted daunting shadows while gliding over a graveyard grass meadow. Dead bodies owned no shadow as the sun sailed the deep blue skies with no paddle. Evening bats rode the last untamed rays of vanishing sunlight while preparing for a wild night. Poisoned four-legged savages laid empty of life, whose bodies will nourish the visiting night. The sun detailed the jungle with delicate strokes of touching light while gently waking the creatures of a restless night. Stealthy scavengers slid from beneath the beds of daytime sleepyheads, who rested their weary heads. Screeching chimpanzees sharpened their spears from stable trees as toxic gas released from the bellies of the deceased. Big-eyed bush babies bolted under the bushes before quietly venturing out again to feed on forbidden fallen fruit.

"I don't get a good feeling about this, dear friend. Do not allow your stomach to get us killed, as you are our leader. Those predatory primates are quite devious and deceitful, so please not be fooled by only mere silence and sudden calmness. Listen to me, Titus!" a frightened bush baby squealed from underneath the safety of a blueberry bush.

"Silence yourself now, Bonjavi, for I hear nothing of your lies. For I must consume the forbidden flesh of a fallen fruit, which all of you are commanded to do as well," Titus squeaked angrily as he hopped into the open and under an enormous shadowing tree.

Fleshy fruit with golden skin twinkled in the drowsy evening as aurum frogs sighted crouching chimpanzees. The gates of Atlantis will close, and the vast blue seas shall turn dry. Titus's big ole eyes opened wide with wonder as he caught sight of the juicy herd of fruit lying in the grass. The greedy bush baby mouth dropped on the ground as he ate the forbidden fruit by the pound. Titus's tummy grew big and round until he couldn't even move around. There were enough bush babies to fill a town, but sadly their numbers were about to be cut down. Heavy potbellies weighed them down as snickering chimpanzees watched from aboveground. Sleepy bush babies closed their tired eyes while staring up at the dreamy sky. Stealthy chimpanzees slid down from slippery vines as they used their spears to dine and wine. Fruit-filled bushmeat piled high in the chimps' empty bellies as bloody apes speared all who ran. A squirming galago's head was ripped off by the might of a mighty ape's hand before its plump body was emptied like a soda can. The mini red-eyed primates bounded across the grassy moss-covered forest floor as they retreated from a team of herding chimpanzees. An ambush of searing spears skyrocketed in temperature until plunging into the bloody bodies of fat hollering bush babies.

Waking stars looked down in sorrow as their troubled eyes twinkled in a troubled mind. Blood soaked the tear-stained grass while golden frogs hopped on a moss-covered log. Black-haired savages preyed on the weak, like bumbling cowards who do not believe in a final judging Higher Power. Babies crawled from beneath their dead shielding parents, like infant sea turtles escaping their sand-filled coffins. Spiraling spears stabbed the squealing fur babies as they attempted an escape to a dense sea of blueberry bushes. Spirit-calling coyotes welcomed the wild night, like blood-crazed devils singing out of sight. Darkness poured from the heavens as angels turned off the lights. A wandering night butterfly rested atop a sitting brown-eyed gorilla, whose blinded sight only saw the blackness of night. Forbidden golden fruits littered the crime site as shadow creatures stormed a mourning night.

C H A P T E R 5

Fire-lit flies danced in a ballroom of darkness as they glowed under a bloody red moon. Golden frogs leaped toward happiness before being weighed down by the weight of a dying world. A gentle silverback gorilla sniffed his dark hand while picturing a black butterfly fluttering in this stolen land. The sweet-hearted ape's chocolate eyes melted with joy as his loving soul momentarily pulled back a blinding curtain. An old gorilla's pearly smile of white gems beamed in the opaque night until dark wings turned into a blinding cocoon of light.

"So you've been returned back to us, for the creatures of this land have endured many years of hardship and sorrow. My unsighted eyes have witnessed the rebirth of a true king, who is protected by the chief of angels and his divine army. Look at the light, my mute brother, who hears perfectly and speaks many languages with his hands. For you must pass the message on to our deaf brother so he may bear witness as well. So hurry along now, Ram, and find our wise younger brother, Be," the blind gorilla said calmly as a bursting cocoon of light erupted atop his flat midnight palms.

A giant gorilla galloped gracefully into the deep dense jungle until later arriving with his deaf younger brother. Gobbling gophers tunneled underneath the blood-soaked ground while moving around with no sound. A battle-scarred nighthawk viewed down from atop a dead tree as a precious stone bled red underneath the blood moon. Moist golden-skinned frogs ribbited underneath a moss-covered log while hiding away from the sight of hungry eyes. Searing light exploded in the blind ape's charcoal palms as a man born of the stars walked out unharmed. His hair was like the head of a lamb, which was soft to thy hand. A man birthed from a star, whose body reflected the starry night sky. Galaxies twinkled in his never-ending eyes as fresh air gave breath to a man so wise. His body was molded within the heart of a great Northern Star, who watched His divine creation from afar. The tall young man's skin shifted from an indigo sky to an all-black man hide, which bore many tiny burning stars inside.

Starlight burned deep within the starlit man, who smiled down at his trio of gorilla friends. A shady nighthawk lurked the shadows before nabbing a gold frog without a paddle. Flaming pink flamingoes groomed the water with their bent bills as a blue pat passed over deep blue waters. A flock of blue flamingoes complemented the night sky, like homemade gravy on steaming white rice. White mice stood baffled outside the barrier as a blinding light took all of their evil sight. As only those with the eyes of our Creator can endure, for His creations possess this planet's divine light. Twisting turtles twisted their terrible night away as cheerful otters sang the hate away. Blood drained into the soil and clay, which stained Mother Earth's breaking heart away. Negro wool hair locked over broad shoulders as a calming breeze cooled his boiling blood.

"Oh, my dear Pardis, you've grown to become such a strong leader, just like your powerful father, who gave his life for this land. My spirit has told me of your destiny, and even the answer which you've come to seek. Now is the time for you to speak, my young king, for we've seen many things in our old lives," the blind gorilla voiced deeply to his night sky-skinned levitating friend.

"I desire to leave this barrier, but your help is needed in order to do so. Use your unique gifts to create an opening in this barrier's soft center, so then my freed soul can bring peace to our wild land. May you lend me a helping hand, as I'm only a shape-shifting man with different skin," Pardis said passionately while slowly rising higher toward the crown of the towering trees.

"True power resides within you, my king, as a Higher Power channels His spirit throughout your specially designed body. We are only mere warriors of prayer, for you walk with the chief of angels. You need no help escaping this barrier, but we shall pray light into this dark situation, my dear king," the blind gorilla said tearfully while grasping both of his brothers' gentle giant hands in united prayer.

"Do you know why we pray in a triangle of three?" Be asked softly.

"No, I do not, my deaf brother, who listens to the movement of the lips. Inform me of your unique method of prayer, for I am very unaware, and this news must be shared to those in great despair," Pardis responded to his ground-dwelling spiritual brothers, who formed a triangle of locked hands.

"We pray in the shape of a mighty mountain, for only a mountain can move a mountain. May the Most High bless and protect you on this dangerous journey as we shall pray for your safe return, my king," the blind gorilla said sincerely before calling upon his guardian spirits and briefly whispering words in an unknown language.

"Fear not, Harambe, for I walk heavy in the footsteps of divine Father!" Pardis bellowed to his blind gorilla friend, who gave a gentle smile to the man above.

The burning eyes of angered angels watched over their enslaved ancestors, whose memories had been wiped clean of a spiritual past. Midnight coyotes conversed with higher spirits while singing ancient lyrics of change and destiny. Chanting gorillas casted out evil with words of peace and forgiveness, for our enemies know not what they do. Their sincere prayers revealed the puppeteers of this world's hidden scheme of mass manipulation, who intend to cage and harvest all descendants of fallen angels. Amber firebugs swarmed the praying great apes as unwavering faith forced mountains to crumble and humbled wicked storms. Ancient spirits inhaled the chanting gorillas' blue aura before raising them high into an ember-eyed night sky. The barrier's protective skin painfully peeled back as powerful prayers pushed up toward the peaceful heavens. An indigo streak of passionate light bolted into the healing chest of Gabriel, who delivered a sincere prayer message to the throne of our Creator. Pelting rain weakened the enchanted barrier, thus providing the heaven-sent lad a grand escape.

"Pardis! You must rush toward the indigo beaming light, which shines down from Heaven. This purifying light comes from the raging star, who burns far up north. Follow this vertical tube of healing energy, as it will rebirth you into a powerful force. Your journey must not pass three days because then the enemy may infest our untouched land. Our lives lay in your chosen hands, so please do not fail to heed these warnings. Convince the Aduboola to leave without struggle because refusal shall result in their own destruction. Midnight hands will stain with the blood of all enemies while protecting those who piece together your broken heart. Pardis, you must save our Night and Day people, who respect the land and understand their place in this life. Bring back all of the imprisoned wild things, for their untamed souls must roam this world free. Shackles and chains weigh down both of our kind, like a drowning boat filled with squealing swine. Hurry now, my king, for time is of the essence!" the unsighted gorilla said with burning passion while gently being lowered down to the ground by gargantuan helping hands.

Tall trees reached for the starry sky before bringing down the elderly prayer warriors. Flaming stars burned holes into the Earth's sleeping blanket as Pardis's heart shined through his galactic chest like a sun trapped in a skintight vest. Balls of fire floated in space, like lost spirits drifting in oblivion. No man has stepped on the moon, for I know life is nothing but a mere cartoon. They distract you with trips to the moon; meanwhile, they groom our children for doom. Galaxies swirled on the star-jeweled man's gifted body as he swiftly maneuvered around sturdy trees in vicious flight. His long deadlocked hair harnessed the strength of a mighty lion before exploding into a grassy savanna and leaving the ancient jungle behind him.

"I must save all who will follow me, for Death is expected to be born soon. We must take safety underground, just as our ancestors have done in the past. Mass destruction is in the near future, for I sense spiritual devastation for those who do not value life. Peace and harmony will exist in the underground city of Atlantis, which is where we shall reside. Opposers will flee to the mountains, like scared rats evacuating a flooded bottomed-out world. I am the link between my human and wild beast brothers, which is why I've been chosen by Noah to lead his ark. Fear not, my indigenous and innocent creatures, for true power owns not one face!" Pardis voiced with a burning heart as he and the ground quickly began to depart.

Pink-feathered flamingoes caught wind as a powerful galactic being transcended into the vast starry sky. An open mouth of a falling waterfall drooled over smooth rock as angered spirits commanded water to flood the world. Rushing agua carried life through the dying Earth, like blood flowing veins in a cancerous body. The stealthy leopard silently crept toward a herd of sleeping gazelle as Pardis glided soundless over its lush green grass heaven. Lone trees sprouted sparingly from the ground, like living limbs of a perishing planet. Sleepless stars counted the leaping gazelle as a soul-snatching feline dragged its kill into a watchful tree. The spotted leopard's golden eyes flickered in the masking night as it crouched atop a rare acacia tree. Freshly squeezed blood dripped down to the traumatized ground; meanwhile, laughing hyenas cackled in a dark background. Smooth rainbow rock signaled to the stars while standing behind a youthful waterfall. Spiritual koi fish swam against a furious river, who fought them every step of the way on their spiritual journey. Ancient glowing-eyed crocodiles protected a sacred river of eternal life as an indigo light shined bright over falling water. Traveling toxic air tainted a beautifully painted landscape once the enchanted barrier began to open its soft center. Pardis plunged into healing waters of an ancient place after taking the form of a dark-scaled koi.

Troubled waters tested his determined spirit as he journeyed atop a falling mountain of water. Onlookers from other worlds cheered with joy once the black koi awakened his heaven-sent strength. Pardis leaped over exhausted bodies of colorful fish, who lost faith and plummeted back down to the deep dark depths of a drowning depression. The dark-bodied koi kissed the moon before transforming into a legless feathered dragon. Sapphire eyes twinkled in the night as white feathers ruffled during flight. The mighty dragon's long open snout consumed deep breath wind as bloody red teeth put fear into hearts of unseen evil spirits. A fearsome crown of golden antlers blessed the blue blood dragon as he escaped his home's magical barrier with great ease.

"This false world shall crumble at the fury of my Creator, for they have made themselves gods in the eyes of lost men. The Most High will instruct me to herd His selected sheep before destruction blooms in this stolen land. My people remain imprisoned for false crimes. Meanwhile, they commit unholy acts behind closed enemy doors. The floodgates of Atlantis shall close as water shrivels on the sand. Oceans will become dying deserts in a forbidden land as food of the sea shall sicken all of man. No more will they rule a stolen land, for the black king has taken the stand. I walk with archangels, who lead my way. They protect me from danger every single day. This world is not ours, but for now I must stay. As I'm commanded by High Powers, who cannot be seen with your eyes, will we run and die like slaves today? Because I come to fight my demons, who've been warned to stay away. Good mingles with evil every single day, which always why I pray. For now, peace and tranquility trick them to stay, almost like a passing tiger who has overstayed his stay. Famished wolves reclaim their taken land, for the enemy must not stay. I command the wolves who survive today to chase that not so welcomed tiger away, so our children might own this stolen land one day," the blue-eyed feathered dragon growled while wrapping a full bleeding moon.

CHAPTER 6

I'm dying inside,
Living and withering at the same time,
But not even my loved ones can hear my desperate cries.
I stay strong and wipe my teary eyes,
For I'm a visitor from faraway skies,
Sent here to keep lost souls from burning in eternal fire.
I speak truth,
But the enemy has fed you all lies,
And to that I must cry.
Those whom you love the most
Will laugh and watch you die,
Mines watched me burn in the fire.
No helping hand given to I,
Until the Most High said rise.
Like a burning phoenix,
Whose loving heart has been burned from all sides.
So today I might go outside
To escape the demons who hide inside,
Heart murdered by loving those who've fed me lies.
My soul is immortal,
So me and Death shall not lie.
Black boys of the humid night
Dance under the stars who shine so bright,
Their pained eyes twinkle with love and delight.
Bravehearted warriors,
Who are tough to fright,
Hence the reason they beat us all day and night.
I panic in the sweaty night,
For my soul has awakened with terrible sight.
Eyes wide and filled with a haunting fright,
I turn on the lights.
And there lies the terror of the night,
Black skin sewn to me very tight.
See, I remember now, alright,
Because that just happened last night.
My spirit tells me to rest

And only venture out at night.
For evil seeks to steal my divine light away
As a creature of the thieving night.
You must live to avoid the day,
I'm sorry for getting carried away.
I guarantee my tongue will stay in its place,
Thank you for listening.
As I tell this story at my own pace,
Brittle black boys danced the eerie night away,
Unaware that traveling evil runs to where they stay.
The whispering wind warned them to run away
And to be weary of where their heads may lay.
But a drunken night turned up his twisting tunes
While shucking and jiving the oppressing darkness away.
Needless not, should I say,
These children did not live to see a new day.
For white horses pounded the ground to paste
As white-hooded heroes made haste to save a screaming damsel
in distress.
Beautiful pale skin complemented her snow-white dress,
Unconscious she lay,
Her tender, sweet body bloodied by merciless rape.
Disgraceful memories of a guilty white gentleman being allowed
to freely run away,
Haunts your beloved grandpa to this very day,
For broke little black boys had to pay that day.
Oh, do I mean in the worst way,
Sickened by what their eyes have seen,
They knew someone must intervene.
So on their own understanding,
Did they lean on?
Yes, indeed.
Now as I proceed on,
I would like to mention.
That there was no lynching!
On this particular day,
For the enemy had other plans this dreamy dark day.
Screaming mothers were raped,
As their innocent sons were violently dragged away,

Before being brutally bashed in the head.
Painting their Negro skin dark bloody red,
White hooded vigilantes tied up the boys' legs.
Loyal steeds raced across rocks and grass,
And occasionally a pile of broken glass.
Bloodcurdling cries escaped the traumatized boys at last,
As their naked bodies were allowed to be dragged,
Until arriving at the alligator-infested swamp,
Where they were hacked and fed as chocolate snacks.
Late nights followed by long black days,
Can lead the most determined soul astray.
Evil lurks deep down south,
I was born at the bottom,
But the top I came out.
Sadness is happiness,
For pain has muted my mouth.

Pale egg-shaped houses littered our Earth Mother's ebony skin canvas, like a growing cancerous rash that has gone unchecked for far too long. Sweltering concrete replaced soft green grass as busy automobiles hurriedly sped past. A herd of toxic clouds suffocated an ill blue sky until every traveling bird had died. Bustling crowds of mindless Aduboola swarmed the filthy streets, like grey-furred mice scurrying from the drowning depths of melting ice. A giant artificial orb shined over their vast city, for Mother Earth's dear warmhearted sun refused to share his light. Invisible beast patrolled the streets as enslaved night and day people waddled barefoot in shackles down a blistering street. Their eyes flickered no more with the Pupil of Life, for they only can now see false light through pained eyes. Chained night people wore skin of those deemed not so bright by those who burn in divine light. Darkness shrouded the Pupil of Life, which once thrived in gifted eyes given to people born of light. Cracking whips cracked down on crying children, whose exhausted little arms could no longer carry their stolen workload.

Invasive Aduboola destroyed the natural world just to only create an artificial hell. Magical temples and teleporting pyramids decorated this once free land but were destroyed upon the abrupt arrival of rat-tailed invaders. Some sacred structures withstood the disastrous invasion, which made them targets to be removed. A man with no past has no future. Thieving Aduboola snatched the golden pen of history after murdering and enslaving an entire civilization of indigenous folk. Innocent blood-drenched pure soil until turning Mother Earth's irritated skin the color of freshly sliced redwood. Some remnants of native history still stood strong in this destructive land, like bloody camelias on a war-torn battlefield.

Dying children of the sun wilted and shriveled up, like dried prunes on a flaming hot sunny day. Their bodies fed off natural sunlight, which was only available to those locked within the enchanted forest walls. Young overworked bodies lay lifeless on scorching pavement before being gobbled up by starving invisible beast. Forsaken orphans harvested vital energy from a bleeding full moon, which blossomed just the other night. Deceased children of a nurturing darkness glowed dark blue, like all departed creatures born under an indigo dipped full moon. Dead bodies were separated by the color of their skin so then selective organ harvesting could begin.

A conspiracy of black hat rats sat amid ancient artifacts while orchestrating their next attack. The top hat rats' fat bellies reflected their bountiful harvest of murdered Day and Night orphans. Shiny black fur complemented a sharp set of gold incisors as treacherous tongues turned their thieving owners into big fat liars. Their grimy pink hands stole secrets of bodies they just happened to acquire while hungry beady eyes watched a sacrificial lamb roast over controlled fire. They were proud owners of the Black Rat Marketplace, who supplied us all with hate.

Plump black rats scurried across crumbling artifacts as scattered remains of a fallen empire were copied and stored in the far back. Whip-wielding Aduboola lashed into turned backs of enslaved blacks after they were caught resting inside the temple. Abusive Aduboola angered quickly after coming in contact with Day and Night slaves. Passing families tossed stones at the heads of beaten and shackled children; meanwhile, predatory male Aduboola preyed on young virgin girls. City lights and toxic pollution blinded the eyes of sad-eyed children, who carried their history to an awaiting demise. Hate burned beneath grey skin of prejudice Aduboola as they stared angrily at the chained natives. Woolen-haired women of the night solicited themselves with shame as they stood naked within dark alleys. Lovely ladies of a slaving Day cleaned wealthy homes before being forcibly raped and beaten to the bone. Mourning indigenous men whimpered while watching their masters play break the buck. Passing vehicles honked viciously as angry drivers attempted to run over stolen slaves of a taken land. Towering egg-shaped buildings looked down upon trudging human cattle, who trekked across an unnatural bustling city. The broken-spirited slaves' beaten backs cried blood as they forcefully hauled off their valuable history into a guarded fenced fortress. Blood, sweat, and tears sizzled atop the burning pavement, for a Negro-winged butterfly continued to quietly flutter on by. Hope opened blinding shutters after sensing her long-lost brother's drifting ghost.

"The black king of this stolen land has returned to save his lost people! Wicked imposters who have imposed cruel treatment unto this beautiful world must pay full price for all they've taken from us. For karma comes to collect payment, which has been long overdue!" an enslaved man of the gentle Night voiced passionately before being released from his cramped cage and dragged to deathly gallows.

CHAPTER 7

Death speaks to the mind of the quiet,
For IT will always move in silence.
The wolves wait behind the beautiful bush,
So do not live naive and blinded,
For I see the sheep have been misguided.
Atop the hill, they've all been sighted,
I'm going to lose my lost sheep,
Due to not being able to speak.
I look up to the deep blue sky,
As I'm in dire need of the Most High.
For a blessing is what I immediately seek,
I pray to own a tamed tongue and soothing speech.

A black-winged butterfly drifted deeper into shadowy depths after being spotted by a bellowing man. Su sangre colored the scorching pavement like a fine red sand. An angered Aduboola soldier palmed the crazed dark man's woolly skull before looping a flaming rope around his neck. Cheering crowds gathered around like a cackling murder celebrating senseless murder. Innocent fellows hung from deathly gallows, for they couldn't be submissive and mellow.

A sizzling evening evaporated blood and tears as droplets of pure hatred oozed from the enemies' boiling pores. An unseen monster stood motionless amid yelling Aduboola, who demanded the life of an outspoken slave. The hanging man of Night displayed no fear before being pushed from atop a deathly gallow. His bleeding legs flailed in thin air after an Aduboola kicked away the noosed slave's wooden chair. A maiden statue wept red tears as she silently watched blood fill the eyes of a hanging dark-skinned man. Invisible beast caught whiff of an unwelcomed intruder, who silently fluttered toward its waiting open jaws. The floating black-winged butterfly landed atop an invisible beast's slimy tongue. Nothing remained of the wandering insect, not even a lost crumb. The hanging slave managed to grab a hold of his custom-made rope before managing to utter last words of hope.

"Death stumbles down upon those who walk in their own

footsteps. Fear not, children of this land, for salvation is almost here. Many of my people have been hung and harvested like slabs of butchered meat. Soon it will be I who you seek, for truth is what we must speak. Slay them all, please, my black king, for I've grown tired of their mocking and laughing. Cut their throats where they stand, then decapitate these treacherous thieves thieving hands. For I'm only a simple man, who was never given a helping hand by those of man. Death rises from the gut of a forgotten beast. Disease shall sail our seven seas until all evil cease to exist," the hanging man uttered to all of his enslaved sistren and brethren, who have given an evil enemy every ounce of their divine hope and love.

"We must silence this untamed slave! For he has stepped over time and continues to dodge the kisses of death!" yelled an angry Aduboola.

"I wish not to be you nor those who follow in your footsteps. For Death will show no mercy, for you've spit in face of the thirsty. I foresee eternal life for those who willingly choose His path. Abandon all of your misguided anger and free me from such a senseless ending. Listen to words spoken by the wise, so then you shall be spared from a terrible demise. You must choose to stand on the right side despite being judged by blind eyes," the slave voiced with a broken heart while preparing to roughly depart to a Great Land blessed afar.

"I choose to follow the way of my fellow Aduboola, who've deemed themselves superior over all lowly creations. So speak to me no more, filthy human, for I hold your life in my bloody hands. Fear me now, slave, before I stick my spear into your weak body," the rowdy rat-tailed humanoid hissed irritably.

"I forgive you for being lost, my brother, but just know that your life choices come with a hefty price. Those dice must be rolled, so advise you to do so. You shall be showed no mercy by Death, for it's time we must depart," the hanging slave voiced with great difficulty while paying close attention to a startled crowd of prejudiced Aduboola.

"How are you even alive? Never mind giving an answer, for my blade shall pierce your foul flesh! Perish now, slave!" the lunging Aduboola bellowed with great anguish.

"My name is Azeil…," a dying enslaved man whispered while smiling into the empty eyes of murderous monster.

"Foolish humans will always die by my sword. Meanwhile, the wise shall serve all Aduboola. Die by my sword or serve me as your lord. I can never change my wicked ways, for this way of life defines me inside and out," the now calmed-down Aduboola voiced with no compassion whatsoever before descending back down to the ground and licking stained blood off his soul-swiping sword.

"You should honor the dead, for everyone must join them someday. I watch through the eyes of an unseen monster, whose primitive mind submits under your damned mind control. Murdering those who oppose a self-proclaimed rule will not bring peace to your tormented souls. I watched you slay my spiritual brother like a squealing pig forced into senseless slaughter. By loving grace of the Most High, another chance has been bestowed down upon you. Do not live the same life of bumbling fools, who are being manipulated like murderous tools. Free all of my people, who operate mindlessly within your unfair society. Heed this warning now, heathens, for a shift in our atmosphere brings change of prophecy. I wish not to end your life, since giving a life is harder than taking one. I pray your decision benefits both of us, my rather ill-tempered friend," an air-cracking voice erupted amid a mob of cackling vermin, whose naked eyes could not witness the beast speaking from within.

"Who speaks to me with lack of fear? Expose this fool, so I may strike him down with ease!" the red-eyed Aduboola hissed angrily.

"None of us have spoken against you, Lord Xon, for we willingly live the life of a true Aduboola!" an ember-eyed female Aduboola shouted abruptly, thus causing the glaring red-eyed mob to cheer with murderous cries.

"Do not question your ignorant followers, Xon, for I'm the true king of this stolen land. Allow your eyes to refocus in center of this crowd as the exposing wind blows away this hiding creature's clever disguise. Now close the mouth and talk with your eyes," a voice growled deeply from within the now visible beast.

Turquoise and violet feathers flirted with a brashen wind, who ruffled the two-legged beast's rather exquisite coat. Emerald green ojos glimmered in the false light like freshly unearthed gems. Flesh-mutilating teeth flared a bloody orange as the barbaric creature stood tall and strong. A long tail whipped violently back and forth; meanwhile, large sickle claws tapped the ground impatiently. Harpy claws were equipped to lighting fast hands, which retracted a gut-wrenching power from a pair of emerald-scaled arms. A grotesque fragrance of rotting human flesh emitted itself from the warm-blooded monster. The beast screamed in deep anguish as an unsettled wind whipped all standing violently back and forth. Fear consumed a once fearless Lord Xon, who groveled on the ground like an abused dog. A lone red scarab crawled from the beast's bottom eyelid while causing its temporary vessel immense pain and suffering. Tiger orange tears streaked down the face of a mentally tortured creature, whose caged mind scratched and screamed for freedom. Inner chains snapped within the unique beast as a bloodied beetle emerged from breathing flesh. A mentally freed slave stood tall and mighty while looking down at his pleading master.

"Allow me to handle these ungrateful heathens, for your purpose is greater than just murder. A great awakening is going to break dawn soon, like a newly awakened black butterfly flying across wakened skies. Heed my burning words, for time is of the essence. You must go awaken the other invisible beast, who patrol these grimy streets all day and night. Those who refuse your offer must be slain on sight, like rabid black men wandering these diseased streets. You will answer to me until our people are all free. A creation breathing without a name has no existence in the naked eyes of the living. Arambu shall be your given name, as of now the chief of angels can fight your enemies from afar. So go now, Arambu, and gather all who are willing. Look to the sky for guidance as you follow a trail of changing lights. This sign from above shall lead you and your followers into the golden gates of Atlantis. So open your eyes wide as I bestow a gift upon thee," the bleeding beetle said passionately before shape-shifting back into his original human form.

"Your eyes possess thousands of stars, which are windows to a spiritual world. Countless galaxies spiral out of control as they attach themselves to your skin and bone. I choose to follow willingly, for you are the sacred black king of this taken land. You are the vessel of many divine Higher Powers, who guide and watch over you during the stormy night. The Creator has chosen you for a divine purpose just as you've selected me. This new power is unimaginable, as my worn body feels reborn again. Thank you for this glorious opportunity of redemption, for my lost soul was doomed to darkness. Failure is not an option! I shall lead my herd to vast blue pastures of the hidden city of Atlantis!" Arambu voiced sincerely before going invisible and setting out to accomplish his divine mission.

"A fox who was raised by savage wolves must learn to hunt and kill evil ghouls," Pardis hissed and growled angrily as his pitch-black body underwent a ferocious transformation.

CHAPTER 8

Vengeful lashing white tails viciously struck the hardened ground like angered bolts of lightning. A violent five-tailed Reynard's murderous inky eyes glared into a terrified crowd of cowering Aduboola. The extreme transformation triggered a raging supernatural storm, which disciplined those below with soul-frying zaps of lightning. Lord Xon pleaded to the sitting snow-white fox, who gave his enemies a bloody smile. La sangre dripped nonstop from razor-sharp teeth as pulses of violent wind escaped its now screaming mouth. Petrified Aduboola looked to their powerless leader for protection but became devastated once discovering his hidden imperfection.

"Lord Xon, the Almighty. Why hesitate on execution of this foul beast, whose risen amid our precious home and threatening our very existence. Have you become a coward in the face of death? I believe your throne should be set aflame, for our leader weeps in face of the enemy. Listen, my fellow Aduboola! For I fear that we must fight in place of our once all-powerful ruler, unless there's another way to defeat this daunting beast!" a male Aduboola bellowed from within the silent and trembling crowd.

"Command the chained humans, for a slave's only purpose is to serve us without care of their very own! We are the superior Aduboola race, who walks atop all walks of life. Fight for your masters, which is the correct action to take! I command you, filthy beast, to destroy this creature or choose death alongside us! For we are your saviors, who provided your race with a divine purpose! Fight for your masters, as if your children were to be beheaded!" a female Aduboola voiced angrily aloud before being pierced through her heart by the creature's electrifying third tail.

"No idol worship on Aduboola shall be able to save you from my murderous wrath. Lord Xon cowers at my feet as his wife was just stabbed through the heart. This self-proclaimed king is nothing more than a mere imposter. The sheep will fall to their deaths as wolves wait at the depths. A blind shepherd who cannot see his path shall lead the herd to their own fiery grave in hell. Murder is the salvation of all evil. For I'll be delivering your damned souls in bulk to the waiting hands of hungry demons. Now die to the tune of falling purple rain as I bestow on you some of my pain!" the five-tailed Reynard voiced deeply with great suffering before engulfing its snow-white body in a melting coat of searing flames.

A homicidal beast of fire stormed the screaming streets as extreme heat torched his enemies' soft feet. Aduboola scurried around aimlessly while frantically wailing their elongated arms around in the air. A flaming five-tailed fox's powerful jaws ripped life from pregnant Aduboola as they struggled to keep up with the fleeing crowd. Mindless slaves stood unharmed alongside burning streets, for they were protected by guardian angels. The murderous wind howled bloody red rum, like a murder of ravenous crows feeding on mutilated corpses. La sangre mixed with purple rain painted boiling streets, as well as deserving victims burned up from their scalding feet. An amber flaming fox danced amid praising flames, like happiness surrounded in its own sea of pain. Nonbelieving Aduboola cowered in terror before being brutally disassembled like traitorous friends deserve to be. Vengeance ached within an orphaned man's burning heart, who bears the skin of faraway stars. Bright blood boiling flames burned pitch-black while crying violet tears. An enraged flaming five-tailed fox's eyes burned like a pair of flickering lanterns while listening to several survivors plead for their lives. The mythical creature's murderous smile revealed a sharp set of bloodied teeth. A stirring wind screamed bloody red rum until Pardis became engulfed in searing black flames. Purple smoke choked life from the sick air as a dark inferno swallowed all of city hall. A levitating black fox burned atop a floating purple cloud of smoldering smoke, which carried him higher than the tallest building. The black flaming Reynard looked up to our heavens before abruptly releasing a hellish scream. Spiraling dark rings of fire grew larger as they transcended to the opening sky. An unknown beast attempted to pry open the heavens. Monstrous hands tore open a bleeding sky as a bloodthirsty monster revealed its murderous eye. The screaming fox's eyes turned inky black as it attempted to open a sacred portal. Truth is hidden under the mask of fiction. I foresee this lost world's looming affliction due to their selfish and cruel addictions. Peace lies in the hands of the gifted.

CHAPTER 9

Float on by black butterfly,
For I know you've come to take many lives.
Beauty is where darkness truly lies,
Evil is who we should despise.
But instead, wickedness is what they glorify,
Many have declared themselves as I.
But pain exist not within their eyes,
Love has withered and died within their misguided lives.
Blinded by the mission of eternal life,
Avoiding the Most High is not very wise.
As we all will have to one day look into those divine eyes.
Running away from time in life,
Is like stabbing Death with a dulled knife.
Fly low, my angel of darkness,
I do not care if they pardon us,
For a blanket of darkness has fallen down upon us.
Fear strikes them,
Causing evil to run far away from us.
Cowards abandoning their own people when times get tough,
The enemies' journey will be long and rough.
As they attempt to hide within the mountain's rocky gut,
Go hide and close that cave shut,
For that mountain shall crumble under a giant's crushing foot.

A dark blaze tormented the sinful below as black butterflies emerged from burning ghettos. Herds of fleeing Aduboola swiftly fled underground, like the Antichrist hiding from an ultrasound. Blood painted a tearing sky dark red after rising to the bleeding heavens. Vengeful lightning zapped all who opposed, thus turning resistant Aduboola into solid stone. Bone-chilling cries froze all who could hear as they stood still like statues of stoned deer. A bloody mouth Reynard violently whipped black burning tails back and forth, like cracking whips of red-faced devils. Searing flames of darkness coated the once white fox. The five-tailed beast floated atop a toxic cloud, whose pure soul had been tainted with disease. Gargantuan giants gathered around a growing portal before attempting to forcibly exit the birthing sky.

Giants shall once again stomp the Earth,
As evil man will crumble back to dirt.
For everyone must receive what they deserve,
I'm just sad to say,
Now it's all of your turns.
Since in the ending days,
All of the world shall burn,
But still man will not learn.
For I've come to warn you all,
A godless empire built so tall,
Must one day take a shattering fall.
The black butterfly will come to kiss you all.

A cracking sky closed its burning eye as fire burned in frozen time. Darkness bandaged the bleeding sky, like beautiful homes built atop slave gravesites. Stars blinked their burning eyes while waiting for an ignorant world's self-served demise. A bloody full moon caused the seven seas to rise until their large bodies lay lifeless and dry. Scorching flames of darkness melted out evil eyes, even those who looked from the sky. A flying invisible beast heard the screaming Reynard's summoning cries, which opened borders between your world and mines.

"Cease this madness now, foul shape-shifter! For I cast victory over my fellow Aduboola by slaying such a menacing beast as yourself! Giants shall never govern these lands again!" a tall man of the Night bellowed angrily while riding swiftly atop his trusty winged invisible beast.

A dark-skinned sorcerer rode his fiery steed, like the dragon riders of the Solomonari. Fire torched the murderous air as a jolt of deadly shadow magic bolted toward an unaware Pardis. The screaming five-tailed Reynard countered his enemies with a blow of equal power. Enormous limbs of impatient giants squeezed through a stretched portal. Pardis continued howling to the breaking heavens while retrieving his attacking third tail. An almost complete summoning was abruptly disrupted after Pardis surprisingly discovered the enemy effortlessly sprinting atop his burning tail. The stealthy assailant bore skin of a cold midnight sky equipped with inky void eyes. A striking black serpent coiled upper half lunged viciously toward Pardis. Poison-tipped, hollow fangs pierced the wide-eyed Reynard's black burning neck. The snake's lower half violently constricted Pardis, thus forcing him to return back to his original form. Blood leaked from Pardis's starry eyes as excruciating pain drained his body of time. The serpent's elongated squeezing lower half continued to tighten, all while remaining attached beneath an attacking assailant's strong chin. Angered giants were slowly sucked back into their black hole as the summoning portal began to close.

"And just who the hell do you think you are? Answer me now dammit, before I rip out your intestines and wrap them around your chopped neck," Pardis voiced angrily, while having an estranged man's black feet perched atop both his broad shoulders.

"My name is Bakra. Your father is my younger brother, whose troublesome spirit still resides within you. I was rightful leader of the Night and Day people, but your father possessed those same damn eyes. Divine eyes given only by the Most High, who rules over our vast universe. My eyes are dark like right now. For my heart was forged by hands stained with hate, and all because of my soulless eyes, the title of king was never mine. I harness no abilities given by the divine, which is why your unique eyes must now be mines," Bakra voiced irritably as his razor-sharp tongue brushed up against the neck of a fearless young black king.

"I know nothing of you, so your life is meaningless to me. A day of reckoning shall come to this very land, for one day, I will become stronger and chop off your filthy hands. I'm unsure of how you've betrayed your people, but just know I'll find out. And once I do, I'll awaken those who've been enslaved by the Aduboola. Then I'll allow them to decide your fate, since you're obviously in cahoots with these nonnative vermin. Release me now, or mercy will not be shown at your death. I must open the heavens and allow fallen giants to reclaim their land," Pardis told the hissing man of night, who bore a deadly fanged serpent atop his bald head.

"I cannot allow your dreams to become my reality, young Pardis, for the Aduboola are pawns of my own game. A man born in darkness must learn to see blind before dying lost in time. The Aduboola are a godless race of greedy fools, who have trampled over many peaceful civilizations. I use dark magic to grant them forbidden technology, and in return, they harvest energy from conquered planets, which is then used to fuel my power. The Aduboola only fear death and those who stand in their way. My magic has made them gods, which defines me as a creator. I'll be taking off your head, since it doesn't matter if you're alive or dead. Those precious eyes will title me most powerful being within the universe," Bakra hissed and growled to a bleeding Pardis, who winced in excruciating pain to the tune of a dancing tongue.

"The stars above must burn in frozen time. For no man's pain can rhythm and rhyme. You're a traitor to our own kind, who will all side me at the end of time. I'm protected by those who cannot be seen. So be wary as you sleep, for the mariposa brings death wherever evil decides to creep. The wicked shall fall sick, as naive sheep are entertained by mere tricks. I believe not even you shall be prepared for what is next to come, my dear Bakra. Death grabs the helping hand of life. Who then saves me from drowning in a pool of raging fire?" the bleeding neck star-bodied black man growled lowly to his dark-hearted uncle right before swiftly shifting into a wingless black butterfly and falling down into dark scorching flames.

A wingless butterfly plummeted down to a burning Earth, who screamed out in the heat of night. Fire merged with darkness, thus creating a living hell on Earth. Burning skyscrapers crumbled as those below wished for a cold summer. An abandoned child poked holes into his lonely heart, thus creating stars to watch over him in the dark. Blood stained the wounded sky as healing stars saved all with time. Bright flames who were pushed into darkness burned like a fire born into a world so heartless. Death dodged the damaged souls of beaten slaves, who stood atop their master's burning graves. A fire-spitting, invisible beast pursued the wingless butterfly as it fell through melting time. Bakra rode bareback atop the vicious winged beast, who was summoned out a hidden land from way far east. The shadow sorcerer leaped from atop his trusty beast in a desperate attempt to grab Pardis's tiny feet, but to no avail. The wingless black butterfly continued to fall many more feet. Black fire punished screaming streets until the helpless butterfly burned to a crisp. Hot ashes flickered like lost stars, who've been frozen in a dark space of time.

"All who oppose me shall burn in a sea of searing flames! Pardis, your death will not be in vain, for I've crowned myself the new black king!" Bakra cackled abruptly while riding his unseen fiery beast into a hungry darkness.

CHAPTER 10

Demons in disguise shall rise with the waking sunrise,
Bloody murder leaks from their bleeding eyes.
In a world full of ignorant flies,
Humanity tends to persecute words given by the wise.
Death has been seen by so few eyes,
It saddens me to see this world's obvious demise.
Look around as you listen with your eyes,
Only a fool could not recognize the signs.
I rise from the ashes.
As the Most High protects me during these hard times.
Children of prophecy are created in the womb of fire,
Many around me are deceitful liars.
Those I love once conspired and burned me with fire,
Kick and stabbed me until I died.
Oh, so how hard did they all try,
But my Father commanded me to rise.
For my paternal father is incapable of looking me in the eyes,
And I now understand why.
For his heart remains lost in time,
I tried to love my mother many times.
But that wicked witch cursed me from behind,
Sticking needles in my back,
And praying sickness on my spine.
But I cackle on the inside,
For I see through the eyes of the night and day skies.
Nothing can be hidden from my eyes,
Nor can I be fooled by any disguise.
Death comes to those who seek my demise.
I come in your sleep and speak to your mind,
Relax your soul.
And allow Death to take away your precious time,
For warnings only come so many times.
The black butterfly will come once no plants will rise,
This beautiful creature is the master's death in disguise,
As all seven seas flood dry,
After flooding has taken many lives.

Sickness seeks those who hide,
Mountains are where they shall hide.
But quaking footsteps of hunting giants,
Will cause even the most feared mountain to crumble and die.
Naked skin will burn,
As wicked hearts are issued their turns.
All meat shall be poisoned,
As plants will all be burned.
Nowhere to run,
No matter which way you decide to turn.
For now, it's all of your turn to burn in a hell well earned.
Madness shall eat the minds of sane men,
For most have lived a life funded by wicked sin,
For we are the leaders of many men,
Who are birthed by strangers,
And abandoned by our own so-called kin.
I write my pain with a blood-tipped pen,
For I've been betrayed by many men.
I whistle to the listening wind,
To bring destruction to those who wish my end.
Honor I live by,
And no man sword I'll die by.
For only with faith,
May the sun wake and rise.
Never spit in the face of a man with no eyes,
Because then you may be cursed blind.
Shelter they will never find,
For this is their final time.
Centuries they've taken from innocent people's lives,
Now my angels tell me it's now their time.

The wandering wind stirred up a smoking pot of flickering ash. Raging flames ceased to exist immediately after a lonely butterfly lost his beautiful wings. To some, magic only exists within mere dreams, but for others, it can be found in many things. A fiery tornado twirled under the false morning sun as Pardis prepared to be swiftly reborn. Clear skies looked down with sweet indigo eyes. As an exhausted Mother Earth took great deep sighs, a burning phoenix stood waist high while withdrawing energy from the waking sky.

Ember-coated wings stretched far and wide, like the mouth of a big fat liar. Falling skyscrapers crumbled atop the graves of detached city dwellers. Egg-shaped homes cracked under pressure as a breaking-dawn sky cranked up the heat. Searing waves of fiery wind torched the bruised ground. Homeless victims screamed aloud after witnessing a burning creature being lifted up with no sound. A screeching phoenix soared high above all below before receiving an almost fatal blow.

"I see you've rejoined the living, Pardis! It's way too bad that you must return back to the land of the dead. For I serve the ruler of Haides, and he's made me superior to all beings. My shadow magic created this handsome wonderland, which you attempted to destroy with a single hand. Luckily, I was able to conserve a small portion of my precious world. But unfortunately, I can spare none of you. For your eyes must be taken, as I will show no pity! Now die just like your weak father!" Bakra voiced with such an evil tone while riding atop his magical fire-breathing beast of the sky.

"Only a fool would step to me as you've done for a second time. Now I call on my angels to lend me power of the Great Divine! For my very own strength is in drastic decline. Kill yourself now, heathen, or be slain like the rest of your own kind. Allow me to show you why I am the true black king of my own time!" an injured Pardis voiced deeply before swiftly shifting back into his original unique human form.

"I would rather be devoured by wicked demons, who freely roam the uncharted depths of my very own soul! You shall die by the twisting tongue of my hissing bow!" Bakra shouted back hastily, not even realizing this would be his final punch.

"Well, so be it then, for I'm willing to die over my respect! Do you hear me, Bakra!" Pardis voiced with roaring rage while looking into the eyes of flying death.

Roaring rage ignited stars within their double-spaced cages as Pardis's flickering eyes burned unfazed during these dark ages. Many days had moved on since the star-bodied man was warned by the wise. The gorilla with no seeing eyes looked up to a blue crying sky, for time had passed on by, like an ocean draining desert dry. Most men would rather go blind than see the world through my eyes. I pray for the rain, while others beg to see clear skies. Pure skies shall come once our seven seas turn dry. For all water wishes to float in fresh pools hidden within a deep blue sky. Crazy—no, not I, for I just speak word of the wise. Have you forgotten that some men are blessed with divine eyes?

"A mighty lion never sleeps during a vicious battle! Prepare for a bloody war as I ride with archangels into battle! Blood stains the feet of my loyal stallion, who wears a heaven-sent golden saddle! For my bloody sword shall always draw blood in fierce battle!" Pardis roared with immense power before catching the poison-tipped, serpent-shaped arrow with a free handful of sorrow.

A smoking dragon fell down to earth after being hit where it truly hurt. Poison-tipped fangs drained death into the burning veins of a creature made insane. Great pain flared in the glaring eyes of a child born under a bleeding sky. The Bakunawa lay motionless as its body slowly turned to stone. A calming wind blew soothingly as Death freed the enslaved soul of a monster turned cold. Pardis swiftly followed with a fatal blow after becoming engulfed in an indigo glow. The snarling skull of an alpha Simba swallowed Pardis's dreadlocked head. An armored suit of golden lion bones shielded him as the dragon blew his last hot breath. A cracking whip rapidly wrapped around the slain Bakunawa's frilled neck after igniting into a flaming lion's tail.

"Sever the beast's angry head, only if one wishes it to be dead. Your overgrown serpent has been beheaded, like a greedy chicken laid down for slaughter. Now you shall know the pain of your very own creation!" Pardis growled deeply after using his fiery whip to rip off the dragon's rather large head.

"I will never die alone! Your actions will be paid in the blood of your own kind! May my Aduboola servants worship me at their sacred shrines!" Bakra bellowed with a menacing cackle before launching a destructive arrow of powerful dark magic toward the enchanted forest.

A serpent arrow remained lodged atop the dome of a fierce dragon, who died and turned to stone. The horned beast's severed body lay heavily down upon the crown of sacred ground. Bakra turned and gave a menacing smile after bombing the forest with unimaginable evil. The black snake bit its own tail while performing as a supernatural bow. No stars burned on traitorous skin, for his body was black as an empty night sky. The ground shattered and quaked all around as an indigo cloak manifested into a fierce lion.

Rubble and debris raised off the ground before vanishing into thin air. A burning lion tail whip disappeared but was quickly replaced with deadly claws. Fear wiped across the face of Bakra after sensing his opponent's bone-crushing spiritual power.

"Just what the hell have you become? Answer me now, damn it!" Bakra exclaimed before being savagely ripped into bloody chunks of black meat and devoured by a lion-hearted warrior.

"Those who draw their swords will be slain like those deemed mentally insane, as I'm a beast who can never be tamed. Can you feel my pain now, Bakra? For I, the black king, was forged in a sea of murderous flames," Pardis said with great pain as he grew vast blue wings and took flight to save the enchanted forest.

CHAPTER 11

Forgive them, Father, for all they do,
For they know nothing of all You do.
All would do better if truth they knew,
I understand not the separation of red and blue.
We're all victims of death and very bad news,
So there's no reason to give each other the blues,
For we all were born with our necks tied in a noose.
Red is all my brothers see,
Peace is somewhere they fear to be.
Black bodies drowning in a deep blue sea,
Widowed mothers stuck on praying knees.
Enslaved children caged somewhere they need not be,
For our country only fight false wars overseas.
Ignoring the war between lost blackbirds and stinging bees,
I've seen things that would make you chop off your knees,
And force you to crawl into a bleeding sea.
Can you guess who the real enemy might be?
Can color-blind people finally all see?
For many are lost children cast away into a divine prophecy.
Age matters not to me,
Since this is not the first life,
Which I've been born to see.
Gossiping fools are not wise to me.
Many are deceiving shepherds feeding lies to who they keep,
Two-faced wolves costumed as innocent praying sheep.
Are any of your lost souls even worth to keep?
Single black mothers pray,
As fatherless children weep.
Unlike others who speak,
Death doesn't wake us from our sleep,
For I know you wish our souls to keep.
Lies is what they speak.
Truth is what you seek.
Take a trip to make believe.
Experience many fantasies,
Then your eyes may truly see

Exactly where truth is destined to be.
The spirits are in a rage,
Most of my people dwell inside a cage.
The cruelty we've all endured,
They cannot relate,
But still they hate and lock us away.
Do folks not believe there will come a day
When Death may come and take all away?
No man knows the time nor day.
I pray no more souls are led astray,
As there will come a time,
When the wicked must pay.
I pray all my people will unite someday.
For I come with warning,
During these last evil days.

Natural sunlight blinded Pardis as he swiftly soared toward a dying forest. An army of black ooze devoured all who moved. Harsh screams echoed from within a chaotic jungle as terrified wildlife were quickly escorted into hidden underground tunnels. A team of spiritually awakened beast remained visible while rescuing shell-shocked native refugees. Arambu and a posse of former invisible beast were derailed from their original journey in order to save many innocent lives.

"The dark ooze is consuming more bodies than we can simply save. Trees have fallen into toxic graves as this gluttonous ooze continues on its deadly rampage. I'm unsure of how generous time will be unto us. I fear we must scan this diseased jungle once more. Cerberus, go seek out a sacred trinity of gentle gorillas, for they're precious to my beloved shape-shifting friend," Arambu voiced to a three-headed canine subordinate, who stood tall over his striking battle-scarred leader.

"I shall execute every task given unto me, for my divine purpose is to serve selflessly during this time of awakening. Where might these gentle giants lay down their heads, Arambu?" Cerberus growled in unison to an attentive leader, who used his large sickle claw to orchestrate a message composed of unique taps.

"The enemy listens to our spoken words, so one must move like deer feeding under a harvest moon. Do you understand?" the feathered raptor voiced in a shaky low voice before pointing his winged arms toward an eavesdropping puddle of creeping black goo.

"I see evil listens once others choose to do right. Your message is understood, Arambu. Just know we must escape this cesspool of devouring wickedness before a swallowing darkness engulfs our tired souls," Cerberus told his weary-eyed leader before dashing down the trail given by a signaling North Star.

"The North Star will guide all who seek peace and justice preserved in this stolen land. You must save the Trinity, for they are the last of their kind. Mystical creatures who were blessed to inhabit this bloody planet. But as evil grew from the depths of dark valleys, so did sickness in wise gorilla bellies. Pardis would be devastated if the Trinity were to die, so this is why I must guarantee their safety at all cost!" Arambu voiced irritably as he foresaw a puddle of wicked ooze lying still, waiting for a charging multiheaded hellish beast.

"Unfortunately, Cerberus's hearing was damaged by a whispering witch, so yelling will never alert him to any screaming danger. I must use my lightning speed to save my beloved soldier! My life means nothing if I cannot protect those who are shielded within my bleeding heart!" Arambu expressed with growing vigor before accelerating to speeds faster than a shooting star.

A fiery North Star burned boldly in a dimming blue evening sky. Evil ooze covered the suffocating ground like a black face mask. Trees drowned in gooey darkness, like made-up dinosaurs falling into bubbling tar pits. Dead bodies of innocent animals were rapidly being digested in the belly of a gluttonous evil. Awakened visible beast carefully covered their tracks before quickly concealing the tunnel whereabouts. A red howler monkey melted in a bleeding fire after burning bridges with red-eyed chimpanzees. The stressed ground cracked in two, like a log being axed in half. Arambu awakened an inner power, which gifted him with incredible abilities. The cloak of a flaming golden eagle engulfed the vibrant feathered raptor as his feet skated across untamed air. Arambu became consumed in a ball of raging flames, which grew hot arms equipped with heavy hands. A blazing ball of passionate wildfire grabbed and absorbed every retreating body of living toxic ooze.

"Worry not about me, Cerberus! For the Trinity must be your main focus! Our Earth Mother will not be able to heal without the help of those gifted gorillas! I'll handle this faceless growing blob of hungry evil, so just continue seeking the Trinity!" Arambu screamed aloud from within his massive ball of blazing wildfire.

"I give my sincere word, for in these dark times of man, trust and faith are all we have to lean on until the Creator reclaims this lost kingdom. The Trinity will not be devoured by the black goo, which dooms all who moves. Thank you, Arambu, for you've proven to be a leader worth following and much more. You took upon yourself to awaken all who would listen. So many are on their way now to the hidden city of Atlantis, and all because of you, Arambu. I take great honor in having served under your guidance. May the flames of darkness burn bright in times of a calming coldness," Cerberus voiced unto himself after being set free of a swallowing goo of wretched evil.

A bravehearted beast charged into the burning heart of a diseased forest. Hungry black goo crawled for the shadows before being snatched up by hot hands of an untamed inferno.

Striking serpents viciously defended their three-headed host, who frantically sniffed out his hiding targets. Bloodred snakes bled at the mouth while being attached all over a bloodthirsty hellhound. Cerberus's thick black fur stood frozen stiff as air-cracking snakes whipped the attacking black blob. The multiheaded hellhound possessed reddened eyes, which reflected an unimaginable pain tucked deep inside. A green fire began to glow within the unlit area of dimmed forest. *El verde* flames erupted from within volcanic pores, which covered Cerberus's hard body. Chaos drooled just outside the front door of peace, for blue magic struggled to protect three dying gorillas, who became sick from so much impurity in the world.

"We must go now, or the black blob will consume us all!" Cerberus growled to a trio of dying apes, who huddled together sick and barely functional.

"Pardis, is that you, my dear child?" Harambe asked softly.

"I'm afraid not, dear blind elder, for my name is Cerberus. We must go now, since others wait on our arrival." The three-headed monster answered before retracting his bloody snakes back into their fleshly host.

"I am truly grateful to you, my dear Cerberus, for you possess a heart forged of pure gold. I can't help but to wonder on the whereabouts of our beloved Pardis. Have you been in contact with him recently?" the blind gorilla said faintly.

"Yes, he awakened me in the middle of city hall. They were hanging slaves from the gallows, and then Pardis arrived in disguise. He ordered me to free all willing invisible beast and to return back to Atlantis. Me and the others were on our way there until we caught wind of this attack. Many decided to continue on with their journey to Atlantis. We are the few of many who are here to save innocent lives," the multiheaded hellhound voiced before grabbing all three elderly gorillas with gentle monstrous jaws and storming off to Atlantis.

"Pardis is the child of prophecy, so we must leave this battle in His hands. He is a warrior of the Most High and a king to those like you and I. The life force of that despicable Lord Xon has vanished from within this realm. Bakra also seems to have been defeated by a crushing opponent. Was Pardis responsible for their departures?" Harambe said with a very faint voice.

"The war has begun, my blind elder, which is why we must abandon this stolen land. We must find the hidden city before time runs out of patience. Pardis has defeated all who opposes the natural law of this once free realm. He is destined to rule this land again as our devoted black king," Cerberus said to a now unconscious blind gorilla, who dangled from the racing hellhound trio of drooling jaws.

The bright evening turned depressed as night slowly approached. Angels peeped into the sad world of enslaved mortals, like stars watching over us as we slumber. The wind carried the scent of others, who continued on ahead in pursuit of Atlantis. Cerberus sniffed the air vigorously while following a trail of tail tucked cowards.

"The others must have encountered some difficulty because I sense less living bodies than previously. They deserted their own family and friends just to reach a place of underserved peace. Cowards deserve not to be saved but slain like pacifist wolves. A sword who doesn't kill in battle will eventually shatter under the molding pressure of life. The good always die young while trying to protect cowards who stand up for nothing right. Is a fool's life worth saving? Why risk your existence to spare the lives of such selfish beings? Am I a coward for leaving Arambu to fend off the enemy? I believe my strength is much needed to protect my friend!" the three-headed beast said within his own heads before coming to a sudden halt amid a valley of shadowy darkness.

"You better not look back, Cerberus! For my raging flames will not discriminate and may turn you into solid stone! Continue on the journey blessed down upon you. The North Star shines over you, my beloved comrade. So trudge on, brother, who's lost in the blinding night. Loving light shines bright at the end of every tunnel plagued in darkness. A fool is simply a fish who has chosen to dwell at the filthy bottom. A wise man swims against falling water. All knowing the strength he'll gain by having a journey given much harder. We are here to serve our divine purpose until the Creator calls us back to Him. Question not who deserves help, for most are simply unhappy faces with many mask. Pray for those who only know how to ask. Forgive those who know not how to forgive others, for they have not forgiven themselves. Learn to love with no expectations, since that is when your heart will blossom under divine light. Once you learn how to forgive all, then many blessings shall and will fall. Now hurry on to safety because I sense my end has come. Give them all what I've given unto you and forgive them even if they're not forgiving to you! May my inner fire light up this dark world! A confusing place where so many sane men are driven to a world of blinding madness!" Arambu's voice echoed under a falling of blanket darkness, which burned like a house set on fire in the deadened night.

Indigo flames merged with the wild child, who wielded a fiery spirit made of searing blood fire. The hungry night's stomach boiled with hot temptation as it circled the perimeter of a dangerous burning sensation. A *rojo y azul* inferno of peaceful flames incinerated every blob of remaining evil black ooze. Tears tumbled down the cheeks of a crying triple-headed *perro*, whose sweet prayers were heard by a dying moon. A moon who once gazed happily down on a honeysuckle sweet meadow but now weeps at night in a world that never settles. Death of a moon delivers flooded meadows and bodies afloat in forgotten ghettos. Never shall the sea ever settle as long as two-legged beings continue to meddle.

Cerberus carried the unaware Trinity bravely into a sea filled with purple rain. A road leading unto Atlantis was paved by those who remained saved. These beautiful divine beings dedicated themselves to freeing their enslaved loved ones of all kinds. A cloak of protectant blue magic shielded Cerberus from every drop of evil, as he traveled down to where most would drown in a sea lost in time. Running water trailed behind a charging beast as he descended down into a valley forged so deep. Cerberus bounded down watery steps of falling water while trying not to view back at the ones burning behind him. Arambu joined the ranks of the Most High's sacred angels, who willingly held up a violet falling sea. Cerberus raced deep down toward the guarded gates of Atlantis as his past burned swiftly away to ashes. A begging light got the attention of a heroic man, who flew in the body of an indigo lion. His roaring golden skull ripped through the air like a stomach-rumbling pride of mighty Simbas.

"The beating heart of a burning soul can fight all darkness. Divided we fall, and together only can our heads stand tall. Then blinded eyes of naive souls can truly see the truth-telling light, which only a clear conscious sky can humbly behold. Arambu, I sense your fiery spirit amongst my army of guardian angels. My spirit tells me that many lives were saved despite how wasteful hungry evil behaved at a helpless dinner table. A serpent-faced arrow poisoned my bloody heart. So now, who will save me from the bleeding dark?" Pardis said passionately to himself as his heart turned cold within a falling body of heavy stone.

Made in the USA
Columbia, SC
01 February 2025

52567924R00036